Create the
perfect gift!
With 70+ stickers,
wrapping paper, gift
card and envelope.

Tear out this page
so that the next
page becomes your
new front page.

For my amazing dad

Finish the picture of your dad by drawing his hair and maybe glasses or a hat.

Love from

. . . .

Your hobbies

The things you love doing are:

- ⭕ playing games
- ⭕ gardening
- ⭕ watching TV
- ⭕ fishing
- ⭕ cooking
- ⭕ watching sport
- ⭕ playing golf
- ⭕ reading
- ⭕ ....
- ⭕ ....
- ⭕ ....
- ⭕ ....

Tick the boxes and add some more hobbies, then use stickers and draw your dad doing his favourite things.

Off the hook!

Here is a story I wrote about
our fishing adventure.

....

....

....

....

....

....

....

....

....

....

....

....

....

Write a story about what would happen if you went fishing with your dad.

All about Dad

The country you were born in is called ....

Your favourite colour is ....

The colour of your eyes is ....

The colour of your hair is ....

The pets you had when you were little were ....

....

Your favourite animal is ....

The food you like most is ....

When you relax, you ....

You get cranky when ....

Fill in the blanks with what you know about your dad.

Dad's the word

I think you are:

- ○ tall
- ○ funny
- ○ hairy
- ○ neat
- ○
- ○
- ○
- ○

- ○ nice
- ○ messy
- ○ short
- ○ loud
- ○
- ○
- ○
- ○

Tick the boxes and add some more words that describe your dad.

Superhero Dad

Create your own cool comic strip of you and your dad by filling in the word balloons.

Green thumb

Finish drawing the sticker people to show you and your dad in the garden.

This is a picture of us in the garden.

You are number 1!

I think you are the best at:

- ⭕ driving
- ⭕ cooking
- ⭕ sports
- ⭕ telling jokes
- ⭕ singing
- ⭕ _____
- ⭕ _____
- ⭕ _____

- ⭕ shopping
- ⭕ eating
- ⭕ riding a bike
- ⭕ building cubby houses
- ⭕ _____
- ⭕ _____
- ⭕ _____
- ⭕ _____

Tick the boxes and add some more words.

Dad display

Here are some pictures
of my favourite things
that we have done together.

Draw some of the cool things you and your dad have done together in the picture frames.

Dad's day out

One day, Dad and I went to .... We got there by

.... When we arrived, we were surprised that

.... But very soon, we could see ....

Dad yelled out, '...'.

I tried to .... but couldn't quite make it.

I said to Dad, '...'.

'...' he replied.

Suddenly, ... then I saw

.... I got closer to find that

....

It wasn't long before ....

We quickly .... Luckily for us

.... What an amazing day!

Fill in the missing words to create an amazing story about you and your dad.

Radical ride

Draw your dad a cool new ride! Maybe he would love a rocket ship or a shiny new boat?

Happy Father's Day!

Here's a present
I drew for you.

Draw a special present for your dad.

Tie-rrific!

These are some ties that I designed for you.

Colour in some colourful ties for your dad.

My favourite things

I love it when you help me to:

○ Ride a bike

○ Paint pictures

○ Play tennis

○ Play games

○ Go swimming

Tick the boxes, draw and use stickers to show your favourite things to do with your dad.

Kicking goals!

I think your favourite sport to play is ...

You are good at playing ...

I could beat you at ...

Your favourite sport to watch on TV is ...

While you watch the TV, you snack on ...

Your favourite team is ...

Draw or use stickers to fill in the answers.

BBQ bonanza

If I made you a BBQ dinner, this is what I would cook for you.

Draw some BBQ food on the BBQ. You could add sausages, steak, onions, burgers, whatever your favourite BBQ food is!

Dad's den

These are the things that you would have in your secret hideout.

In the thought bubbles, draw some of the things your dad would have in his secret hideout.

Funny face fun!

Here are some of the
funny faces you make!

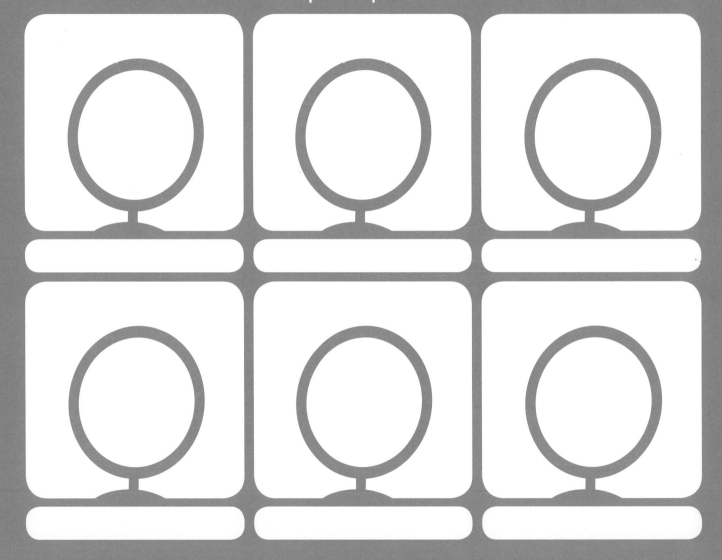

Draw some of the different faces your dad makes and describe them underneath each picture.

Family fun

Here is our family on
a picnic in the park.

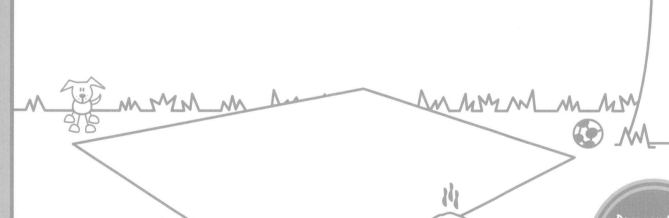

Draw and use
the stickers
to finish the
park scene.

Your castle

Here is the sandcastle
we would make together
at the beach.

Draw an amazing sandcastle on the beach.

And I love our family!

Use stickers or draw your family in the picture.
Write their names underneath.